P9-CQL-513

PINEHURST ELEMENTARY SCHOOL
P. O. BOX 97
PINEHURST, IDAHO 83850

gr. 1

The Bouncy Baby Bunny Finds His Bed

by Joan Bowden

illustrated by
Christine Westerberg

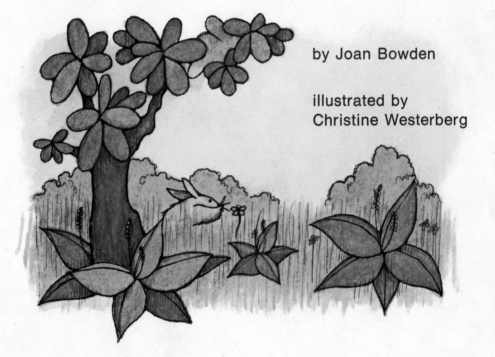

 GOLDEN PRESS
Western Publishing Company, Inc.
Racine, Wisconsin

© 1974 by Western Publishing Company, Inc.
All rights reserved. Produced in U.S.A.

GOLDEN, A LITTLE GOLDEN BOOK®, and GOLDEN PRESS®
are trademarks of Western Publishing Company, Inc. No part
of this book may be reproduced or copied in any form without
written permission from the publisher.

Second Printing, 1976

Every morning, way back in the woods, the bouncy baby bunny had fun playing with his brothers and sisters. Then down, down the hill they would go, roly-poly-over. The bouncy baby bunny was always in front—the first one to tumble into their hole for an afternoon nap.

But one afternoon, the bouncy baby bunny simply could not get to sleep. He fidgeted and fudgeted, and he wriggled and wiggled, until THUMP! WHUMP! BUMP! He kicked his brothers and sisters out of bed!

The other little rabbits didn't like it, not one bit. "You are too bouncy for us," they said crossly. "Go and find some-place else to sleep!"

So that's just what the bouncy baby bunny did.

He found a beaver's home. But it was not as comfortable as a nice, dry rabbit burrow, and he could *not* get to sleep. He fidgeted and he fudgeted, until SPLOSH! SPLOP! SPLAP! He kicked all the little beavers out of bed and into the beaver pond.

Mother beaver didn't like it, not at all. "You are much too bouncy for us," she said crossly. "Please find somewhere else to sleep!"

So the bouncy baby bunny tried napping with the chattery chipmunks where the cattails grow.

He tried snoozing in a field mouse's house where the pussy willows blow. But each time, he ended up kicking his friends out of bed.

The animals didn't like it, not even a little bit! "You are much, *much* too lively for us!" they cried. "Scoot! Scat! Shoo!" And they chased him away.

The bouncy baby bunny felt very sad. He wished he were in his own snug home. *But—*

At that very moment, back at the burrow, his brothers and sisters were wishing the same thing. A mean old skunk had come along and turned them out!

"This is *my* hole now!" said that pesky skunk. "Here I am, and here I'm going to stay!" He rolled himself into a tight little ball (you won't forget this, will you?), and in next to no time, he was fast asleep.

The little rabbits tried and tried to get that mean skunk to leave. They tried being nice: "Mr. Skunk, would you please go away?"

They tried being nasty: "Go away, skunk, or we'll eat you up!"

But that old skunk wasn't even listening. He just rolled himself into an even tighter ball (you *won't* forget this, will you?), and in next to no time at all, he was faster asleep than ever.

The little rabbits didn't know what to do next. Oh, how they wished that their lively little brother were there to help them. *But—*

At that very moment, in an old hollow log on the top of the hill, the bouncy baby bunny was visiting a porcupine.

The porcupine was not at all cuddly, but by now the bouncy baby bunny was very, very sleepy. Soon he was snoring—but not the porcupine!

The porcupine simply could *not* get to sleep, with a funny little bunny snoring in his house. So he fidgeted. He fudgeted. He wriggled. He wiggled.

Then, before the bouncy baby bunny knew what was happening, OUCH! OUCH! OUCH! OUCH! He himself was kicked out of bed!

Out of the hollow log he rolled, and he went roly-poly-over, faster and faster, all the way down the hill, until—with a WHISH! and a WHOOSH!—he shot right through his own front door!

And with a WHISH! and a WHOOSH! that pesky old skunk, who was still curled up in a tight little ball (you *didn't* forget this, did you?), was shot straight through the back door.

He rolled over and over, down the hill, and ended up smack-dab in the middle of a brambly bush.

Quick as a flash, all the little rabbits hopped back into their hole. And the bouncy baby bunny called, "Here we are, skunk, and here we're going to stay! Go away, and don't come back!"

That bruised old skunk was only too pleased to go away from a baby bunny so bouncy he could even kick *him* out of bed. He ran and ran, up and over the hill, and never came way back into the woods again.

As for the bouncy baby bunny—how glad his brothers and sisters were to see him again! "You are not too bouncy for us, after all," they said. "You are exactly right!"

The bouncy baby bunny was so full of happiness that he just *knew* he was going to burst. *But—*

At that very moment, he fell fast asleep instead.